Slinky Malinki catflaps

Lynley Dodd

Gareth Stevens Publishing
MILWAUKEE

122 061

The house was asleep.
It was silent and still,
with flickering shadows
on ceiling and sill.
Slinky Malinki
was cozy and snug,
curled in a ball
on the raggedy
rug.

He opened an eye,
inspected his toes,
and washed from his tail
to the tip of his nose.
He wiped 'round an ear
with a delicate paw,
and
S T R E T C H E D
as he silently slipped
through the
door.

Whiskers all twitching
and eyes shining bright,
he SQUEEZED
through his catflap
and into the
night.

He prowled 'round the garden
and smelled every smell,
from the rambling rose
to the snail in its shell.
Then . . .
with a curious,
questioning call,
he sprang to the top
of the tumbledown
wall.
"Prrrr — owp?"
he called.

Out of a bush
at the end of the wall
came two creeping shadows,
one big
and one small.
Slipping and slithering,
scrambling down,
were Greywacke Jones
and Butterball Brown.

Next to the hole
by the tunnel house door,
furtively lurking
were two shadows more.
Up through the leaves
of the five-finger tree
climbed Pimpernel Pugh
and Mushroom Magee.

Down on the grass
by the cucumber frame,
mysterious figures
were playing a game.
They tumbled and chased
with a scuffle and cuff —
the Poppadum kittens
and Grizzly MacDuff.

From nooks
and from crannies,
from mischief and game,
from every corner and crevice
they came.
They sat in the moonlight's
silvery glow,
hobnobbing happily,
ten in a
row.

BUT
out of the hedge
by the rickety seat,
disturbing the birds
in their feathery sleep,
something was sneaking
on pussyfoot paw —
the cranky
and crotchety
SCARFACE CLAW.

Then,
all at once,
came the EARSPLITTING sound
of a caterwaul symphony
echoing 'round.
"Brrrr — owwwWWW
YEEE — OW!
Brrrr — owwwWWW
YEEE — OW!
SSSSSS — pittapit
FSSSSS — pittapit
WOW — YEEEOW!"

It woke all the neighbors.
From window and door
came bellowing shouts
and a furious roar.
"SSSSSSHHHHHH!"
they all said,
"What a RACKETY bunch!
STOP THAT COMMOTION
AND GO HOME —
AT ONCE!"

With a grumbling growl
and a scuttle of paw,
off and away
galloped Scarface Claw,
and
down from the wall
with a hiss and a spit,
went Slinky Malinki,
lickety-split.

The others all followed
until there were nine,
trotting behind
in a tail-waving line.
Whiskers all twitching
and eyes shining bright,
they SQUEEZED
through the catflap
and out of the
night.

The house was asleep.
It was silent and still,
with flickering shadows
on ceiling and sill.
Slinky Malinki
was cozy and snug,
with all of his friends
on the raggedy
rug.

They sat in the firelight's
welcoming glow,
hobnobbing happily,
ten in a
row.

For a free color catalog describing Gareth Stevens Publishing's list of high-quality books and multimedia programs, call 1-800-542-2595 (USA) or 1-800-461-9120 (Canada). Gareth Stevens Publishing's Fax: (414) 225-0377.

GOLD STAR FIRST READERS

A Dragon in a Wagon	*Hairy Maclary's Showbusiness*
The Apple Tree	*The Minister's Cat ABC*
Find Me a Tiger	*Schnitzel von Krumm Forget-Me-Not*
Hairy Maclary from Donaldson's Dairy	*Schnitzel von Krumm's Basketwork*
Hairy Maclary Scattercat	*Slinky Malinki*
Hairy Maclary, Sit	*Slinky Malinki Catflaps*
Hairy Maclary's Bone	*Slinky Malinki, Open the Door*
Hairy Maclary's Caterwaul Caper	*The Smallest Turtle*
Hairy Maclary's Rumpus at the Vet	*Wake Up, Bear*

Library of Congress Cataloging-in-Publication Data

Dodd, Lynley.
    Slinky Malinki catflaps / by Lynley Dodd.
      p. cm. — (Gold star first readers)
    Summary: Slinky Malinki hobnobs with nine other cats in the moonlight, until the cranky and crotchety Scarface Claw disrupts their gathering.
      ISBN 0-8368-2249-8 (lib. bdg.)
      [1. Cats—Fiction. 2. Stories in rhyme.] I. Title. II. Series.
    PZ8.3.D637Sle   1998
    [E]—dc21   98-23890

North American edition first published in 1999 by
Gareth Stevens Publishing
1555 North RiverCenter Drive, Suite 201
Milwaukee, WI 53212 USA

First published in 1998 in New Zealand by Mallinson Rendel Publishers Ltd., Wellington, New Zealand. Original © 1998 by Lynley Dodd.

Printed in Mexico

1 2 3 4 5 6 7 8 9 03 02 01 00 99